The Clue in the Secret Passage

Written by
Glen Robinson

Book 7
Created by
Jerry D. Thomas

Pacific Press Publishing Association
Nampa, Idaho
Oshawa, Ontario, Canada

Edited by Jerry D. Thomas
Designed by Dennis Ferree
Cover art by Stephanie Britt
Illustrations by Mark Ford

Robinson, Glen, 1953-
    The clue in the secret passage / written by
Glen Robinson ; [illustrations by Mark Ford].
    p.   cm. — (The shoebox kids ; bk. 7)
    Summary: When DeeDee and her family go
to stay at her ailing grandmother's scary old
house and their treasured family Bible is lost,
the ensuing search leads to some discoveries
about past race relations in Mill Valley.
    ISBN 0-8163-1386-5 (pbk. : alk. paper)
    [1. Mystery and detective stories. 2. Chris-
tian life.   3. Haunted houses.   4. Afro-
Americans.]   I. Ford, Mark, ill.   II. Title.
III. Series.
PZ7.R56615C1   1997
[Fic]—dc21   97-10454
                                        CIP
                                        AC

97 98 99 00 01 • 5 4 3 2 1

Contents

Other Books in
The Shoebox Kids Series

Hi!

Have you ever explored a really old house? Old houses can be very interesting—and dangerous! Just be sure that it's safe before you explore.

The Shoebox Kids are back! The same kids you read about in *Primary Treasure* are in their seventh book. This time, DeeDee and Jenny are trying to solve an old mystery with the help of DeeDee's grandmother's diary. But they get caught in a new mystery at the same time!

The Clue in the Secret Passage is written by my friend, Glen Robinson. In this story, he shows how valuable the Bible is and what God promises to those who read and study it. When they solve the mystery of Captain Morgan, DeeDee and Jenny learn some important lessons about the Bible.

Reading about DeeDee and the other Shoebox Kids is more than just fun—it's about learning to be a Christian—at home, at school, or on the playground. If you're trying to be a friend of Jesus', then the Shoebox Kids books are for you!

Can you figure out what happened to Captain Morgan and solve the mystery before DeeDee and Jenny do?

Jerry D. Thomas

Book 8, *The Rock Slide Mystery* is coming soon!

CHAPTER 1

The Spooky, Old House

The cold winter wind made DeeDee pull her coat together. She looked up at the old rickety house in front of her. *If I didn't know better, I would think that the house was scary*, she thought. *Most people would think so. It makes me think something else: Grandma.*

DeeDee looked over at Jenny, who stood motionless looking up at the big house. Funny, she'd never noticed before how pale Jenny's skin was. And how big her eyes were. And how she trembled.

"I'm sure glad your mom let you stay over

here with me," DeeDee said, throwing her arm across Jenny's shoulders.

"Is—is this your grandmother's house? It sure is big—and old." Jenny looked at DeeDee, and smiled nervously.

DeeDee shrugged. "Yeah, I guess it looks kind of scary. But my grandma lives there, and she's not scary. She makes the best chocolate chip cookies—" DeeDee's smile faded. "It's just too bad that she's so sick. If she were well, I know she would want to make some for us."

Jenny saw that DeeDee was sad, so she placed her arm across her friend's shoulder. "I'm glad you asked me to come over. With school out and Mom working, it was getting pretty boring at home."

"Come on, slowpokes," said a voice behind them. Marcus, DeeDee's teenaged brother, poked them both in the back. "I've got stuff to haul in here, and you're blocking the sidewalk."

Jenny grinned, and DeeDee laughed as if remembering something. "This old house is just *sooo* neat," DeeDee said. "Mom will be busy with Grandma, so she says we'll have to entertain ourselves. And we will! We can explore the old rooms and play outside. This house is more than a century old. Who knows what we'll find in there!"

The girls stepped onto the big, old porch and entered through the front door. Jenny followed as DeeDee bowed and spoke elegantly. "Welcome to our tour, ladies and gentlemen," she said.

"Hey, I only see one lady here and no gentlemen," Jenny giggled.

"What am I, chopped liver?" Marcus said, coming in the front door with another box.

"You're just the hired help, Marcus," DeeDee said. "You're not on the tour."

"*Sorr-yy*," Marcus said as he disappeared around the corner into the other room.

"To your right, you will see the formal dining room," DeeDee continued. "And beyond it, the antique, but finely preserved, kitchen." Jenny saw a massive wood table with chairs nearest her and an old stove and refrigerator beyond. A small door about halfway up the wall between the two rooms caught her attention.

"What's that little door for?" Jenny asked. "It looks like a doggie door, but it's too high off the ground."

"It's a dumbwaiter," DeeDee said.

"I am not!" Marcus answered from the hall beyond.

"Not you!" DeeDee giggled, and Jenny joined her. Before Jenny could ask what it was, DeeDee opened the small door. Inside was a small elevator with ropes to one side.

"They used to fix food here in the kitchen and put it on the dumbwaiter to send it upstairs. That way people could eat breakfast in bed."

"What people?" Jenny asked.

"This used to be a boardinghouse a long time ago," Marcus said. "That's like a hotel, except a lot of people would stay here for weeks or months at a time."

"Cool," Jenny said. "When did this happen?"

"A long time before even our parents were born," Marcus said.

"Now," DeeDee said, tapping her foot, "shall we continue with the tour?"

Jenny followed DeeDee back to the hallway and across to a dark room with a huge fireplace. "This is what Grandma calls her sitting room."

"It looks like a living room to me," Jenny said.

"Me too," DeeDee said. "But Grandma said you shouldn't call one room a living room. After all, you live in the whole house. So this is a sitting room—where you sit."

Jenny and DeeDee looked at each other, shrugged their shoulders, and sat.

Jenny looked around the room after a long minute. "Can I get up now?" she asked.

"Not yet," DeeDee said. "I have something to show you." DeeDee walked across the room and picked up a heavy, dark object that lay on a table.

"This is the most valuable possession our family has," she said, carefully carrying it back to Jenny.

"It's a Bible," Jenny said, as she recognized it. "And it looks like it's falling apart."

It was falling apart. DeeDee carefully laid it out on the small table in front of Jenny. As she opened the cover, Jenny noticed that it had been burned around the edges.

"It was the only thing that my great-grandfather was able to save from a fire that burned down their house before they lived here." DeeDee said. "Ever since then, it has been called the Family Treasure."

"*Wow*" was all Jenny could say. DeeDee opened the Bible to the first few pages. Jenny saw the date 1899 written on one page. Then DeeDee opened it to a page that listed a bunch of names that looked familiar. Then Jenny realized where she had seen it before.

"Adams—that's your name."

DeeDee nodded. "This page tells when every person in my family was born, baptized, married, and died. It goes all the way back to my great-great-grandmother. Look—" Jenny looked where DeeDee was pointing at the yellowed page and saw that DeeDee's name had been written in the book, along with her birthdate, and the date last year when she was baptized.

"It's got other neat things in here," DeeDee said. "Back here in the back, Grandma keeps her favorite pictures, including a picture of me when I was a baby. Look at this." She showed Jenny a photograph of a young man in an army uniform. "This is my uncle Herman. I never met him," DeeDee got very serious. "He died in a war before I was born. This is the only way I know about him."

"I can see why you call this the Family Treasure," Jenny said.

"DeeDee," a voice called from the other room.

"Yes, Mom," DeeDee answered.

"Marcus left one last box of groceries in the car," Mrs. Adams said, wiping her hands as she came out of the kitchen. "Can the two of you bring it in? Marcus is busy."

"Sure," DeeDee said. "Come on, Jenny."

DeeDee told Jenny about the rest of the house as they walked out to the car. "Only two bedrooms are being used right now. And they're both downstairs. Since Grandma can't go up and down the stairs anymore, she doesn't use the bedrooms up there. We get to sleep upstairs in the room where my grandma slept when she was a little girl," she explained. "There's a big oak tree right outside the window. It's my favorite room in the whole house."

Jenny nodded.

"We used to have to watch out for rats and mice around here," DeeDee said. "We brought a cat in for a while, but Grandma started sneezing. I think she's allergic. Now Dad and Marcus put out traps to catch them."

"Rats?" Jenny gulped, as they grabbed the box and lifted it from the car. "Rats? How big?"

"Oh, not real big," DeeDee said. "They're

really just a little bigger than mice. But once I thought I saw one about a foot long. Dad said I was imagining things." She shook her head. "I hope he was right."

"I don't like rats—or mice," Jenny said in a very small voice.

"We probably won't see either one while we're here," DeeDee said. "Besides, they're busy hiding because they're more afraid of you than you are of them."

"I doubt it," Jenny responded.

"Here you go, Mom," DeeDee said as they carried the box into the kitchen.

"Thanks, girls," Mrs. Adams said. "Now go play. And DeeDee—please be careful with that old Bible. We wouldn't want anything to happen to it."

"Yes, Mom," DeeDee said. "We'll put it away right now."

Jenny followed DeeDee into the sitting room, where DeeDee suddenly froze with a puzzled look on her face.

"What's wrong?" Jenny asked. DeeDee looked at the couch where they were sitting, at the table in front of them, and then over in the corner. *What is she doing?* Jenny wondered.

Then she realized that the Bible was nowhere in sight.

"It's gone!" DeeDee wailed.

CHAPTER

Saving Captain Morgan

"What do you mean, it's gone?" Jenny gulped. "We were only away for a minute."

"Just what I said—it's gone," DeeDee answered, the sound of worry in her voice. "Do you see it anywhere around here?"

Jenny shook her head. "It couldn't have just walked off. It has to be here."

"Did you see me carry it into the other room or outside?" DeeDee asked. "Maybe I did and don't remember."

Jenny shook her head again. "We looked at it in this room for just a few minutes," she said. "It has to be here."

But after twenty minutes of searching, they had to give up. The Bible just wasn't there. Jenny saw tears in DeeDee's eyes. She put her arm around her friend. "It's not your fault, DeeDee," Jenny said. "I was with you all the time, and I know that we left it right here."

DeeDee sobbed. "But that Bible is so important to our family. What are we going to do?"

"Do about what?" Mrs. Adams stood in the doorway. When DeeDee saw her mother, the tears flowed freely. "DeeDee, what's happened?"

DeeDee was crying so hard she couldn't speak, so Jenny tried to explain. "When we came back, the Bible was gone."

"There, there, it's OK," Mrs. Adams said to DeeDee, trying to get her to stop crying. "I have to admit that your story is strange, but the Bible couldn't have gone very far." She stroked DeeDee's hair as DeeDee's tears slowed.

"I'm sure it will show up around here somewhere," Mrs. Adams said, as she sat down on the couch beside DeeDee. "Let's see . . . Has Jenny heard the story of this old house yet?"

Jenny shook her head. "Just that it used to be a boardinghouse. Is there more than that?"

Mrs. Adams smiled. "Much more. In fact, you are sitting in one of the most historical houses in Mill Valley. Chances are, however, you haven't heard much about it in your history books.

"DeeDee's great-great-grandfather Abraham Hartford wasn't a very nice man, and he got involved in a lot of bad things. But when he became a Christian, he decided that he wanted to tell others about Jesus. But some of his enemies still tried to hurt him and his family. They even burned his house down. Finally, in 1904, he moved here and became a preacher—the first Black preacher in Mill Valley. Times were hard back then, especially for a Black minister. People were poor, and his church couldn't afford to pay him very much. Fortunately, he had a little money saved up from his life before. He used it to buy this boardinghouse."

"What kind of people stayed here?" Jenny asked.

"All kinds," Mrs. Adams said. "Grandpa Abraham never turned anyone away. At that time, there were a lot of hard feelings between White people and Black people in town. This was considered the part of town where Black people lived. But Grandpa Abraham allowed all kinds of people to live in his house. That's why the Mystery of Captain Morgan happened here, instead of somewhere else."

Jenny and DeeDee looked at each other. "Mystery?" DeeDee asked, no longer crying. "What mystery?"

Mrs. Adams smiled and went on. "In those days, a bad man named Captain Morgan did a lot of business on the river near here. He made his own whiskey to sell, then used the money to buy guns. He sold the guns to robbers and other criminals down south. He made a lot of money, but he made a lot of enemies at the same time.

"One night, there was a big fight in town, and Captain Morgan got shot. He dragged himself to the boardinghouse here and asked Grandpa Abraham for help. Grandpa took him in, even though the town would have been very angry to have a White man in this boardinghouse on the Black side of town."

"Wow," Jenny said. "What happened then?"

"Captain Morgan's enemies looked all over for him," Mrs. Adams said. "But everyone knew that Captain Morgan had always been extra mean to the Black people in town. His enemies knew that he would never come to this part of town to find help."

"Captain Morgan was smart," DeeDee said.

"Yes, his hiding place protected him for a while," Mrs. Adams said. "He hid at the boardinghouse for several weeks. Then one night, he just disappeared."

"You mean, he ran away?" DeeDee asked.

"Well, most people thought he ran away. But there were some reports of strange lights down by the river the night he disappeared. Some people think his enemies finally caught up with him, killed him, and threw him in the river."

"Wow," Jenny said. "And he hid out in this house?"

Mrs. Adams nodded. "In this very house, in the room at the end of the hall upstairs."

"Wow." The girls were silent for a moment. Finally, DeeDee spoke. "If he just disappeared one night, I wonder if he left anything here."

"Well, you two can check the house out in the next few days," Mrs. Adams said. "Just let me know if you find anything." The girls jumped up and ran to the stairway.

"Just keep your eyes open for that Bible!" Mrs. Adams shouted after them.

Crossed Swords

"Hey, DeeDee," Willie called when Jenny and DeeDee walked into the Shoebox the next day. "I hear you and Jenny are staying in a spooky old house on the other side of town."

In their Mill Valley church, the kids DeeDee and Jenny's age have their class in a small room down a long hallway. Their teacher's name is Mrs. Shue (pronounced "shoe"), so they call their room "The Shoebox." And the kids who meet there are called the Shoebox Kids.

"It's not a spooky house, Willie," DeeDee answered. "It's my grandmother's house."

"Yeah, and it's neat," Jenny said. "It's just too bad that we lost DeeDee's grandmother's Bible." Jenny and DeeDee told the others about the disappearing Bible.

"Sounds like you have another mystery on your hands," Mrs. Shue said. "But I am sure their Bible will turn up somewhere."

"We did get to sleep upstairs all by ourselves last night," Jenny said. "And it's even got a room where a pirate stayed for a while."

"A pirate! Cool!" Chris said.

"Well, he wasn't really a pirate," DeeDee said, "but he was a sea captain, and a bad guy—."

"That sounds like a pirate to me," Sammy interrupted.

"Shiver me timbers!" Willie said, trying to sound like a pirate.

"Ship ahoy!" Sammy added, pretending he was holding a sword.

"Har! Har!" Chris said. "En garde!" He pretended to poke a sword at Sammy.

"Here we go again," muttered Maria, Chris's older sister.

"Settle down, boys," Mrs. Shue said with a smile. "Put your swords away, and let's study about swords in our Bibles."

"Swords! Really?" Willie said.

"Sure, Willie," Maria said. "A lot of people used swords in the Bible."

"That's right," Chris agreed. "Remember—Peter cut off a person's ear with a sword."

"And the angel at the Garden of Eden had a flaming sword," added DeeDee.

"And Gideon's three hundred soldiers had swords," Jenny said.

Mrs. Shue nodded. "Yes, there are many stories in the Bible about using swords. That's how people protected themselves in those days. But did you know that Christians have to protect themselves too?"

Chris raised his hand. "I've thought about taking karate. Nobody would mess with me then."

Mrs. Shue smiled and shook her head. "I'm not talking about stopping bullies. God wants you to be a Christian and succeed in life. But there is someone who wants you to fail."

Maria raised her hand. "That's the devil."

Mrs. Shue nodded. "That's right, Maria. Would you read a text for us? And would you pick one of our big, strong men here to help me?"

The words *big, strong*, and *men* stirred the boys in the Shoebox to life. Maria looked from Sammy to Chris to Willie. Each one flexed his muscles as much as he could, trying to look tough. Maria scratched her head and looked at Mrs. Shue.

"Big? Strong? I don't know. Oh well, I choose Sammy anyway."

Sammy raised his hands in victory and walked to the front. The others cheered him.

"Now, Sammy," Mrs. Shue explained, turning him to face the others. "Maria is going to read Ephesians 6:10-17. As she reads on how to defend against the devil, I will cover you with the protection she talks about." Mrs. Shue nodded at Maria.

" 'Finally, be strong in the Lord and in his great power. . . .' "

Sammy flexed his muscles. Maria rolled her eyes and kept reading. " 'Wear God's armor so that you can fight against the devil's evil tricks. . . .' "

"Creepy," Chris said. "It's one thing to fight another person, but how can we fight the devil's tricks?"

"Good question, Chris," Mrs. Shue said. "Why

don't you and Willie come up here and help me show how the fight would go if we stood on our own." Chris walked to the front, and Willie rolled his wheelchair. Each took a place on either side of Sammy.

"Now, Sammy," Mrs. Shue said. "If I were to give each of these boys wooden yardsticks, what would happen to you?" She handed Chris and Willie each a yardstick.

"I'd get pounded?" Sammy said meekly.

"Boys, show him, but be nice," Mrs. Shue said. Chris and Willie pretended to beat Sammy with the two yardsticks.

"Ouch!" Sammy said. "Those pretend whacks hurt!"

"OK, boys, stop," Mrs. Shue said. "Maria, continue reading."

Maria nodded. " 'That is why you need to get God's full armor. Then on the day of evil you will be able to stand strong. And when you have finished the whole fight, you will still be standing. So stand strong, with the belt of truth tied around your waist. And on your chest wear the protection of right living. And on your feet wear the Good News of peace to help you stand strong. And also use the shield of faith. With that you can stop all the burning arrows of the Evil One."

As Maria read the text, Mrs. Shue reached into a box behind the blackboard and pulled out metal armor. She placed the armor around Sammy's hips, legs, chest, and shoulders. Then she took out some oversized boots and had Sammy step into them. Finally, she pulled out a wooden shield and handed it to him.

"Now those guys can't hurt me!" Sammy said.

"Wait, Sammy," Mrs. Shue said. "The text says to put on the *full* armor of God. You're not completely protected yet."

Willie agreed. "Yeah, guy, what if I were to conk you over the head?" He tapped Sammy on the head with his ruler.

"And you don't have anything to fight back with yet," added Chris.

"It's coming, it's coming," Mrs. Shue said. "Maria, read on."

Maria did. "Accept God's salvation to be your helmet. And take the sword of the Spirit—that Sword is the teaching of God."

Mrs. Shue reached behind her again to take a silver helmet out of the box. Sammy put it on.

Then Mrs. Shue gave Sammy an oversized wooden sword that was sharp on one side and dull on the other. Sammy held it high over his head.

"OK, you guys," Sammy roared, "now I'm ready for you!"

Willie and Chris whacked Sammy's armor with their rulers, but Sammy was unhurt. Quickly, Willie and Chris realized that Sammy was more than a match for them. He swung his sword at them, and they finally retreated to the back of the room.

"Come back and fight!" Sammy roared. The rest of the class cheered.

When they settled down, DeeDee raised her hand. "Mrs. Shue, are we really supposed to walk around and look like Sammy does? It might have looked OK back in Bible days, but today it would look strange. What does the Bible mean?"

"Well, look at the verse," Mrs. Shue said. "It says that we are at war with the devil. But there are weapons available, and these verses tell us how they should be used. What do the pieces of armor and weapons mean?"

It was quiet for a moment as they looked at

the verses. Finally Maria raised her hand. "The belt of *truth* and the chest covering of right living must mean knowing right from wrong."

"And the feet are protected by the 'the good news of peace,' " Sammy said. "What do you think that means?"

"Well, we have feet to take us places swiftly," Mrs. Shue said. "Perhaps the verse means that we're protected when we're taking the 'good news of peace'—the good news about Jesus Christ—everywhere as swiftly as possible."

"And then there's the shield of faith," Willie said. "Strong enough to protect you from flaming arrows."

"That's because faith is belief that God will take care of you no matter what happens," Chris said.

"Exactly right, Chris!" Mrs. Shue said.

Jenny waved her hand then pointed at the side of her head. "The helmet of God's salvation must mean that you have to know you are saved and what Jesus has done to save you."

"I know what the sword of the Spirit is," DeeDee said. "It's the Bible."

"How is the Bible like a sword?" Mrs. Shue asked. Nobody answered. "I guess I can't expect you to have all the answers," Mrs. Shue continued. "But that answer is an important one. Think about it over the next week: How is the Bible like a sword?"

"I don't know how to answer Mrs. Shue's question," Jenny said to DeeDee as they left. "How is a Bible like a sword?"

DeeDee didn't answer. She was busy thinking about a "sword" that was still missing at her grandmother's house.

CHAPTER 4

Secrets Discovered

"I don't understand," Jenny said, later that day. "We have been all over this house. We have been upstairs and down. We've looked in the kitchen, dining and sitting rooms, hall, and bedrooms. We've even searched the bathroom. Give me two reasons why we should keep on searching."

"First, the Bible is still missing," DeeDee said, as they climbed the stairs at the end of the hall. "We have a responsibility to find out what happened to it. We know neither of us took it, and it's pretty sure that Mom didn't take it.

Grandma's sick; she couldn't have taken it. Marcus was gone. Where did it go? It had to go somewhere."

"I realize that, but—"

"Second, I really think the Bible is still in this house. There's something about this house that tells me it still has a lot of secrets we haven't uncovered yet."

They stood at the top of the stairs and looked at the hallway facing them. Three closed doors faced them on either side of the hallway. A fat potbellied stove commanded the center of the room. At the far end of the room stood the tall cabinet and small door that was the dumbwaiter.

"I think you're right about the secrets," Jenny said, staring at the room. "But where do we start? How do we discover them?"

"Well, what would real detectives do?" DeeDee asked. "I guess they would look for clues."

Jenny nodded. "Right. I guess we should look for something that is out of the ordinary, something that is different."

"I think," DeeDee said, "that this house is just full of secret passageways."

"Well, what are we waiting for? Let's try to

find them," Jenny said. "Where do we start?"

DeeDee had the answer. "Let's start in Grandma's room."

The two girls went into the first room on the left. It was fixed up like an old hotel room. A high, full-sized bed stood in the middle of the room. The old wallpaper had yellowed, and the paint on the closet door was beginning to peel away. The girls' sleeping bags were laid out on the floor on top of the thick throw rug.

"How about a tunnel?" DeeDee asked, one eyebrow raised. She grinned. "No, I don't suppose there would be a tunnel on the second floor."

"But what about a tunnel in the wall—or in the ceiling?" Jenny said. As if answering herself, she opened the door to the closet and walked in. The closet was empty, and she looked up at the ceiling. "It looks like there's an opening up there, but it's really too dark to tell if it goes all the way through. It seems like this would be a good place to have a secret passageway."

DeeDee looked at her. "You'll need a chair to reach the ceiling," she said, looking around for one. An old rickety chair leaned against one of the windowsills. DeeDee pushed it away from the window, and the wooden trim of the windowsill fell to the floor.

"*Oops*," DeeDee said. "I guess I never noticed that that board was loose before." She bent to pick it up. "Hey, there's something in here," she said, looking in the hole the board had covered.

Jenny came across the room as DeeDee reached into the narrow hole beside the window. Carefully she grasped a small book hidden in the hole and brought it out.

"What is it?" Jenny asked.

"It's a diary," DeeDee answered. "Grandmother's diary," she guessed out loud. Sure enough, when she opened the front cover, she saw her grandmother's name written there.

DeeDee read for a minute before saying anything. "Some of the writing is hard to read," she finally said. "The writing is faded. But look at this." She laid the old diary out on the bed. Jenny looked at the entry dated July 13, 1913:

Daddy brought in a new boarder tonight. This one is a White man. Momma tells us not to tell anyone he is here. We are sure to get into trouble if anyone finds out.

DeeDee flipped a couple of pages, and they read another entry:

I used my secret passage and checked on the strange White man. His name is Albert Morgan, they says. Momma seems afraid of him, but Daddy is taking right good care of him. He says that he can only do what Jesus would do. I don't know why Momma is so afraid of him. But I saw the clothes he came in with—they were bloody!

I don't know if he is a good man or not, because he has had the fever and hasn't said or done anything since he came.

"Secret passage!" Jenny said. "There was— is—a secret passage!"

"And Captain Morgan was here as well!" whispered DeeDee. The girls giggled and flipped through the book some more, stopping when something caught their attention. Soon they heard Mrs. Adams calling from downstairs.

"DeeDee, Jenny," she called. "Dinner is almost ready, but we didn't get the dishes done from this morning. Can you come downstairs and help me with dishes?"

DeeDee looked at Jenny and sighed. "We'd

better go," she said.

"Well, the diary has waited for this many years," Jenny said. "It can wait another half an hour."

DeeDee and Jenny got up from the bed and started out the door. Suddenly Jenny stopped.

"Just a second," Jenny said. "My mom just got me this new watch. I don't want to get it wet." She slipped the watch from her wrist and dropped it onto the top of her suitcase.

DeeDee and Jenny went downstairs and joined Mrs. Adams in the kitchen. They did dishes while Mrs. Adams and Marcus fixed the evening meal. By the time they were done washing, drying, and putting away dishes, dinner was ready.

"Have you girls used the house key?" Mrs. Adams asked, after Marcus asked the blessing.

DeeDee shook her head. "No."

Marcus frowned. "I left it on the table in the sitting room. I went to put it away; it was gone."

Jenny and DeeDee looked at each other.

"You'll know it if you see it," Marcus said. "It's a gold key on a little chain. It belongs to Grandma, so keep your eyes open for it."

"How is the hunt for the Bible going?" Mrs. Adams asked.

DeeDee shook her head. "No luck yet, but we are hot on the trail."

Mrs. Adams smiled. "Well, let me know when you have the treasure in hand."

The girls nodded. "It's a deal," Jenny declared.

Since they went to the store with Mrs. Adams after dinner, Jenny and DeeDee forgot about the diary until they opened the door to their room and turned on the light. There it was, still lying on the bed.

"Let's see what else we can find in Grandmother's diary," DeeDee said.

"Just a minute, DeeDee." Jenny stopped to think. "Where did I put my watch? Oh, I remember—right on top of my suitcase. Oh no!"

"What is it?" DeeDee asked, turning around.

Jenny stood over her suitcase, her face as white as a sheet. "My watch," she moaned. "It's gone."

CHAPTER 5

The Secret Tunnel

"I don't know if I'm more mad or scared!" Jenny said. "First, the Bible disappears, right in front of our noses. Then the house key disappears. Now someone took my new watch!"

"This is really strange," DeeDee said. "Who was here but Marcus, Mom, and the two of us? And we were either in this room or with them the whole time."

"I think we have a thief in this house," Jenny declared. "And I vote we call the police."

"And tell them what? That someone stole an old beat-up Bible, a key, and a kid's watch while we were awake in the same house? I don't think so."

"Well, what do we do then?" Jenny put her hands on her hips and stared at her friend.

"Let's keep exploring," DeeDee said. "This house has a lot of secrets. Maybe whoever's taking our things is using the secret passage. Maybe we can catch them or find where our stuff is hidden."

"OK," Jenny agreed. "Let's start with that closet. I just know it's hiding a secret passage."

DeeDee grabbed the old chair from the corner. "We need a chair to reach the ceiling," she said. "Help me move this one."

Together, DeeDee and Jenny dragged and pushed the chair into the closet. When it was in place, Jenny dug through her suitcase and found the flashlight she had brought along. She stepped onto the chair and reached up as high as she could, but she still couldn't quite reach the ceiling.

"What now?" she asked.

DeeDee thought a moment. "Let me get on the chair with you. I'll boost you up to the opening, and you can look and see if there's anything up there."

After DeeDee climbed onto the chair with

Jenny, Jenny lifted one foot and stepped into DeeDee's cupped hands. DeeDee lifted her hand up until Jenny's fingers could just reach the edge of the hole.

"Hold on for just a second," Jenny said. She lay her flashlight on the upper edge of the dark hole and grabbed the opening with both hands. "Now push!"

"Jenny, the chair's leg looks awfully wobbly!" DeeDee said. "You'd better hurry up!"

Just as those words left DeeDee's mouth, she heard the sound of wood cracking. Suddenly there was no chair under her.

"*Eek!*" DeeDee screamed. She fell against the side of the closet then hit the floor. "I think I'm OK," she said, "but the chair is in pieces. Are you OK, Jenny?" DeeDee looked around, but didn't see her friend. "Jenny, where are you?"

"Up here," Jenny answered. She was still hanging from the hole in the ceiling. "How do I get down?"

"Hold on just a second," DeeDee said, pushing the broken chair out of the way. "Now drop!"

Jenny hesitated a second then dropped to the floor. The two of them looked at each other and giggled.

"Why did you come back down?" DeeDee asked. "I thought you would climb on through."

"Well, while I was hanging up there, I realized that if your grandmother was a girl like us, she probably couldn't climb into her ceiling like this either," Jenny said. "The opening had to be easier to get to than this."

"Maybe we are doing this the hard way," DeeDee said. "We've got the diary. Maybe it tells us where the secret passage is."

Her words were answered by a rolling sound. Both girls looked up at the hole to the attic just in time to see Jenny's flashlight roll away from the edge. Then they heard it drop some- where.

"Well, now we have no flashlight," Jenny said.

DeeDee and Jenny went back to the diary. They flipped through many pages that were faded and impossible to read. Then they opened to August 1:

I sneaked in to see Captain Morgan tonight. He is a good man; I believe that. He's done bad things before, but Daddy is reading the Bible with him every night. His wound is getting better, and soon he will be able to go outside.

A week later, DeeDee's grandmother had written:

August 8: Tonight Captain Morgan told me about a bad thing he did to a Black family down in Mississippi. He burned their house and killed the daddy. He is real sad about it now, especially because Daddy told him that other White men burned our house before. Captain Morgan said he loves Jesus now, and he wants to do something for this family.

Finally, the girls found one more entry that was not faded:

August 11: I lost my Captain Morgan, but Jesus will take care of him now. I will miss him. Henry did stay with us, like Captain Morgan promised, but he has to stay in the cellar, Daddy says. If people see Henry, we will get in trouble. I sneak down to see Henry every night. I love Henry, but I love Captain Morgan more. Goodbye.

There were no more entries in the book. DeeDee closed the diary and rolled over on the bed to look at Jenny.

"So Captain Morgan did die," DeeDee said.

"How sad. It sounds like Grandma really loved him. They must have taken him down to the river and killed him like we heard."

"Who's Henry?" Jenny asked. "The diary talks about Henry staying in the cellar."

"That's the basement," DeeDee said.

"That's what I thought," Jenny said. "But who was there? Maybe Henry was one of Captain Morgan's—another sailor, maybe."

"I don't know who Henry is, but I do know I am getting tired," DeeDee said.

"Yeah, if I had my watch, I could tell you how late it's getting," Jenny said. "But I don't."

"We'll look for your watch tomorrow," DeeDee said, yawning. "And for Henry." The girls put their pajamas on, said their prayers, and climbed into their sleeping bags.

"Good night," Jenny said, switching off the light.

"Night," said DeeDee, yawning again.

Jenny lay awake listening to the wind blow through the branches of the old oak tree outside the window. Then she heard another sound. It sounded like fingernails scratching slowly across a chalkboard. Something squeaked.

Jenny sat up suddenly. What if it was a rat?

"DeeDee! DeeDee! Did you hear that?"

DeeDee's response came back slowly. "Did I hear what?"

Jenny was wide awake. "I heard a rat. At least it sounded like a rat."

DeeDee rolled over. "I didn't hear anything. Now go to sleep."

Jenny took a deep breath and lay down. "I was sure I heard a rat," she said, mostly to herself.

Jenny was just about to drift off to sleep when she felt DeeDee shaking her awake.

"Jenny! Listen!" Jenny shook the cobwebs out of her mind and listened. Off in the distance, she heard a tearing sound. Then a muffled voice. Then something banged.

Jenny turned over and looked in DeeDee's direction. And immediately she noticed something strange.

"Look!" she said, grabbing DeeDee by the shoulder. The two of them looked across the wooden floor to the base of the far wall. Where the wall and the floor met, a line of yellow light shone toward them.

"Where's that coming from?" DeeDee asked. "There's no door on that wall."

"It must be my flashlight that rolled around in the attic," Jenny answered. "It's inside the wall! It's showing us where the opening to the secret passage is!"

Jenny and DeeDee crawled across the floor on their stomachs to peer into the tiny crack where the light shone through. DeeDee studied it closely before she finally said something.

"Look, there's a little door here. It's been wallpapered over. But if this is the bottom of the door, it should open if we pull it—here!"

DeeDee dug her fingernails into the wallpaper at a point about a foot above the floor. The wallpaper pulled apart easily, and the hidden door opened.

Dust and cobwebs greeted the girls, and DeeDee coughed a couple of times. But immediately they saw Jenny's flashlight shining at them about eight feet down the narrow crawl space.

"Well, what are we waiting for?" DeeDee said. "Let's follow it and see where it goes!"

CHAPTER 6

Dangerous Passage

DeeDee shook her head. *I don't like tight places. I don't like dust and dark. And I really don't like cobwebs. And I am the one saying we should crawl into this hole in the wall? I must be crazy!*

"What are we getting into?" she muttered to herself, as she led the way into the secret passage in the wall of Grandma's old bedroom. "Jenny, I'm glad you made us change out of our pajamas and put on our jeans and sweatshirts. This passage is dirty." She pulled cobwebs out of her hair and tried to fan away the dust.

"I can't see anything back here," Jenny said, on her hands and knees, behind DeeDee. "Your body is blocking the way to the light."

"At least you're not getting cobwebs in the face," DeeDee said. She stopped and picked up the flashlight. "I'm glad your mom suggested that you bring a flashlight." She shone it back over her shoulder at Jenny.

"Me too," Jenny said. "Whew, it's dusty in here. Do you think your grandma crawled through the dust every time she came through here?"

"I don't know," DeeDee responded, "but the diary says that she came to Captain Morgan's room just about every night. If she came through here that often, I would think that would keep the cobwebs and dust cleaned out." DeeDee shone the flashlight ahead of them into the darkness of the cramped space.

"What are we looking for?" Jenny asked. "I mean, I know we're looking for the lost stuff, but where do you think this passage will lead us? Just to another room?"

DeeDee thought for a minute. "I don't know. This is my first real mystery without the rest of the Shoebox Kids along. The boys or Maria always seem to take over. Now it's just us."

Jenny grinned behind DeeDee as DeeDee moved forward again. "Well, I think it makes this mystery kind of special. Even if we don't find anything else, it's still been neat. We found an old diary—and a secret passage!"

Jenny paused. "But you know, we really don't have any proof that your grandmother used this passageway. This could just be something left when they built the house. How do we know anybody has been here before us?"

DeeDee stopped again and shone the light all around. "Look, there's your proof!" She shone the flashlight at two letters and a number carved into the wood above their heads: A.H. 1913.

"'A.H.'! Don't you see?" DeeDee said. "Abigail Hartford! That's my grandmother! Her name wasn't Adams until she got married."

"And those are the same years as in her diary." Jenny rolled over on her back and looked at the ceiling. "That was the year Captain Morgan was here." She looked farther down the passageway. "But look—there are more markings up ahead."

The two girls crawled ahead, and soon DeeDee

saw what Jenny was talking about. Other people had marked their initials on the sides and ceiling of the passageway.

"Look at this one," Jenny said, pointing at some scratches on one side that read: 'R.E.C., 1859.'

"Wow," DeeDee said, looking around. "Here's another one," she said, pointing at one that read, "E.S., 1861."

"Do you realize how long ago that was?" Jenny said. "What were all these people doing in this passageway in those days? Do you think they were people living in this boardinghouse? Or maybe smugglers?"

DeeDee thought for a moment. "My father told me about something called the Underground Railroad that was sort of like smuggling back before the Civil War," DeeDee said. "The slaves who were in the South would run away and try to escape to Canada. People in the North would help them get there and hide them along the way."

"Are you thinking that this was one of those hiding places?" Jenny asked. "That's really amazing."

"But most of the slaves didn't get to go to

school at all," DeeDee said. "It's strange that they could mark their initials on the wood this way."

"Maybe whoever lived here taught them how to write their names—or just their initials," Jenny said.

"Maybe so," DeeDee said. "Anyway, it looks like the passageway is turning ahead of us."

"Good," Jenny said. "I don't like small, dark places."

"You either?" DeeDee asked, surprised.

DeeDee stopped just before the passageway made a right turn.

"Why are we stopping?" Jenny asked.

DeeDee shone her light to the right. Jenny could see that a door with old rusty hinges was attached to the wall. "I think we are at Captain Morgan's room." DeeDee said. She pushed, but the door remained closed.

"Push it again!" Jenny urged.

"I'm trying!" DeeDee said with a grunt. "I guess it's stuck."

Jenny slid forward as much as she could, and the two of them pushed on the stuck door. Finally, there was a tearing sound, and the girls spilled out into the floor of another room, their flashlight clattering ahead of them.

"Where are we now?" Jenny asked, wiping the sweat and dust from her face and hair. She climbed the rest of the way out of the secret-passage entrance.

"Captain Morgan's room, I guess," DeeDee said, retrieving the flashlight. "Hit that light switch by the door over there."

"No, wait," Jenny said. She walked over to the window and looked out over the backyard to the river beyond them. "That must have been what your grandmother and Captain Morgan saw when they looked from these windows."

DeeDee joined her. "I wonder if Grandmother saw those strange lights down by the river that night from here."

"You know, we said that Captain Morgan probably got killed," Jenny said. "But maybe he got away. Maybe he was well enough to escape down the river."

"Maybe," DeeDee said doubtfully. "But what about where Grandmother wrote that Jesus was taking care of him now?"

Jenny shrugged. "Maybe she just meant that Jesus would have to watch over him wherever he went."

DeeDee paused. "What about Henry? Who was Henry? Why did they put him in the basement?"

"You know, I've been thinking about something," Jenny said in response. "Grandma said she snuck down to see Henry all the time. And those people who hid in the secret passage had to have a way to get out of the house without being seen."

"So?" DeeDee asked.

"So there's got to be other secret passageways."

DeeDee snapped her fingers. "There has to be one to the basement, so she could visit Henry."

"And another that let people leave the house secretly," Jenny added. Suddenly, she turned and looked at DeeDee. At the same time, DeeDee turned to look at her. "The dumbwaiter!" they both said at the same time.

DeeDee laughed. "I just know the dumbwaiter was part of Grandmother's secret passage-way through the house. Come on." She started to the door to check the dumbwaiter in the hallway, but Jenny stopped her.

"Wait. I don't think that's the way your

grandmother would have gotten into it," she said.

DeeDee waited. "Why not?"

Jenny explained. "She said she 'sneaked' down to see Henry. If she went out into the hallway, anyone could have seen her."

DeeDee nodded. "You're right. And I think the door to the dumbwaiter is too far off the ground. She wouldn't have been able to climb into it in the hallway." DeeDee turned and looked back at the secret passage. "So, do we have to go back in there?"

Jenny nodded. "I think this passage will lead us to another entrance to the dumbwaiter."

DeeDee shivered. "Are you sure?"

Jenny smiled. "So your grandmother really is braver and more daring than you are?" she asked.

DeeDee's head snapped up. "No way," she answered with a grin. "Come on. Let's get going."

"OK," Jenny said as she headed to the little doorway. She grabbed the flashlight from DeeDee as she passed her. "But it's my turn to be in front."

The girls climbed back into the passageway

and continued on to the right. The tiny hallway went straight for another six feet before turning right. DeeDee huffed as she followed Jenny on her hands and knees.

"Now I know about the dark you were complaining about," DeeDee said. "All I can see is the back of you. Hey, watch it!" DeeDee ran into Jenny as she abruptly stopped.

"End of the road," Jenny said, squeezing herself flat against the side so DeeDee could see. The narrow passageway stopped with a black open space in front of them. Two ropes crossed the space from top to bottom.

"It's a good thing we had this flashlight," Jenny said. "If we had been going in the dark, I would have crawled right off into space."

DeeDee looked more closely at the ropes. "It's the dumbwaiter," she announced. "Now—do we go up or down?"

"Down is where Henry was supposed to be," Jenny said. "Up may be the escape route for the Underground Railroad."

DeeDee nodded. "We need to stick together," DeeDee said. "We only have one flashlight."

Jenny agreed. "Right. Now, how do you call for this little elevator?"

"I think you are supposed to pull on those ropes," DeeDee answered. She slid forward to help Jenny pull the ropes. The girls pulled on the left rope and heard something moving in the elevator shaft below them.

"Here it is!" Jenny announced when the box came into view. "But it's too small!"

DeeDee frowned. "I see what you mean. The dumbwaiter was only intended to carry food. I guess Grandmother could fit if she curled up in a ball. But only one person could fit inside." She thought for a second. "One of us will have to go first and then the other," she decided. "I'll go first."

"But we only have one flashlight!" Jenny cried. "I'll have to wait in the dark!"

DeeDee could tell that Jenny was afraid. "Maybe we should go back and find another flashlight."

Jenny took a deep breath. "No, we're too close," she said. "You go ahead and take the flashlight. I'll wait and follow."

DeeDee nodded and climbed into the small elevator. She shone the flashlight back at Jenny. "I think we should go to the attic first," she said. "I'll send the elevator back when I get up there.

You climb in, and I'll pull the elevator back up. All you'll have to do is hold on."

Jenny nodded. She watched as DeeDee pulled on the rope and the elevator took DeeDee and the light up the elevator shaft and out of sight. But a feeling of panic crept into her mind as the darkness covered her. *It's just like being in my dark room at home,* she told herself. *It's not any different.* But the scared feeling didn't go away.

After a few very long minutes, Jenny could hear the rope swaying back and forth. She put out her hand and felt them. The ropes began to slide through her hand, and she heard the dumbwaiter moving down the shaft toward her.

"*It's about time,*" she muttered to herself, as the elevator slid into position. She climbed into the cramped dumbwaiter space and waited. Nothing happened. Then she heard DeeDee.

"It's stuck," her muffled voice said. "The elevator rope is stuck. Help me pull it."

Jenny reached over and grabbed one of the ropes and began pulling. *It is stuck,* she thought. *The rope must have come off the pulley.* She and DeeDee pulled for a long moment before Jenny felt the elevator begin to move again. *At last!* she thought.

Suddenly she felt the elevator jerk to the side, and one edge of the dumbwaiter came up.

"Wait a minute, wait a minute!" she yelled up to DeeDee. But DeeDee kept pulling.

Twang! Jenny heard something snap, and the elevator began sliding down. "DeeDee," Jenny screamed. "I'm falling!"

The elevator picked up speed as it dropped into the darkness below.

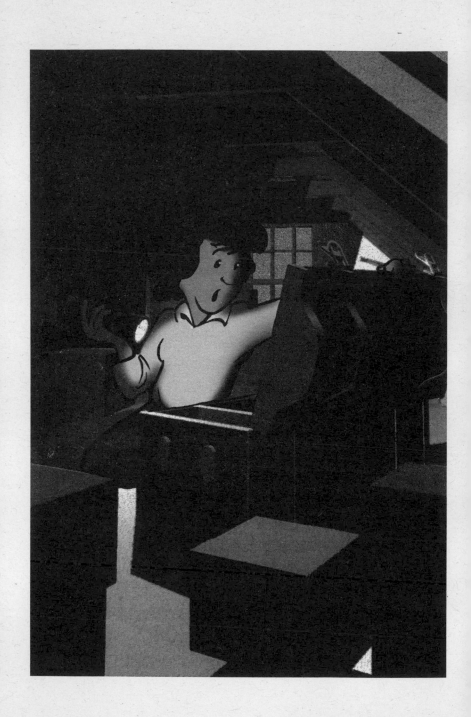

CHAPTER 7

Lost in the Darkness

DeeDee had been pulling on the dumbwaiter rope when she heard one of them snap and the elevator fall down the shaft. She heard wood break as the elevator hit something at the bottom. Dust blew up the shaft at her.

"Jenny!" DeeDee yelled down the shaft of the dumbwaiter. "Jenny!" For a long time she heard nothing. Finally, she heard Jenny's muffled voice.

"I'm OK," Jenny shouted. "It was a scary ride, but I'm OK."

"Where are you?" DeeDee yelled down the shaft.

"I can't tell," Jenny shouted back. "It's pitch black down here, but I think I'm in the basement."

"Do you think the elevator will work?"

"No," Jenny answered. "It's broken."

"Do you want the flashlight?" DeeDee asked.

"Then you would be in the dark. Isn't there a light switch down here or something?"

"There should be," DeeDee said. "See if you can find it. I'll try to find a way out of here. If I can, I'll get help for you."

"Good luck," Jenny voice said from below.

"We don't need luck, Jenny," DeeDee answered. "Jesus and His angels are with us."

Dear Jesus, DeeDee prayed. *Jenny is probably very scared right now. I know I'm scared, and I have a flashlight. Jenny is all alone in the dark. Please send your angels to help her. Amen.*

DeeDee stood up and shone her flashlight around the dark attic. The beam from the flashlight reflected off cobwebs that hung from the wooden beams above her head.

"Ugh, more cobwebs," DeeDee said out loud. *God, why did you create cobwebs?* she asked inside her head. "Probably to keep girls like me from going into scary places like this," she answered out loud.

She continued to flash the beam of the flashlight around the room. *Not much up here*, she thought. She had expected the room to be full of boxes and trunks that would provide clues to the house's secrets. Instead, she found that it was almost empty.

Then she noticed that there was a small window on the far side of the attic. She walked over to it and looked out. A full moon shone outside, and she could see trees swaying in the wind. The window looked big enough for a person to climb out. *Did the hiding slaves climb out of the attic here and then to the ground using one of the oak trees?* she wondered.

She started to open the window, but it was nailed shut. *Someone didn't want me to climb out on the roof*, she thought. *I'm kind of glad I can't. It's cold out there.*

She turned and looked around the room again. The light from the full moon shone into the far corner, and DeeDee could just make out a large object that she had not seen before. It was nestled deep in the corner, almost out of sight. As DeeDee shone her light on it, she realized it was very large, about the size of a large dog.

I wonder what it is? she thought as she took a couple of careful steps forward. *I'm feeling a little nervous up here all by myself.* As she got closer, she saw that it was covered with a heavy canvas cloth. *What could it be?*

Slowly she walked across the attic until she was within a few feet of the big object. The ceiling slanted down near the edge, so DeeDee had to scrunch down to get closer. Finally, she could reach it.

She quickly realized that the shapeless canvas covering had been tied over the top of the object with a piece of wire. The wire had gotten rusty. It didn't take much effort for DeeDee to bend the wire so it came apart in her hands.

Moving the heavy canvas off the top of the object was a bigger problem. DeeDee had a hard time finding a way to grasp the canvas. It was heavy oilcloth, and her hands couldn't find anything to hold onto. The edges of the canvas were tucked under the object, so she had no way to pull it off. Finally, she pulled one edge loose. By pulling it up and away, she was able to work the heavy cloth off the top and push it back behind the object.

"It's an old trunk," she said out loud. It was

square on all four sides and rounded on top. "And it's big enough for Jenny and me to both fit inside." She shone her flashlight at the trunk, and the brass corners, hinges, and latches shone in its light.

"Wow," she said in a half-whisper. On the front of the trunk were two initials: A.M.

"This trunk must have belonged to Albert Morgan—Captain Morgan." She looked at the huge latch in the front with its giant lock. "Should I try to open it? I'm sure it's locked up tight. A man with as many enemies as Captain Morgan would have always kept it locked."

DeeDee reached over and tugged at the lock. To her surprise, it fell open. *Do I dare open the trunk?* she wondered. *I have to—the answers to a lot of our questions may be in here.* Without waiting another second, she flipped the center latch up, turned the two side latches, and pushed the lid open.

As the lid went up, DeeDee's mind was racing. *What could be inside? Treasure? Guns? Captain Morgan's whiskey?* But the first thing she saw was just everyday clothes folded neatly inside the trunk. She carefully lifted shirts and pants from one side and placed them on top of the others on the other side.

Beneath them she saw a layer of books. "*Inland Navigational Techniques*," DeeDee read out loud. "That must be about sailing a boat on a river." The second book she picked up was called *Shallows, Shoals, and Safe Harbors Along the Lower Mississippi*.

"I was right—books about sailing on the Mississippi River. Well, they look boring to me," she muttered. She looked at the titles of a few more before setting those aside. Next, she saw a small white box.

She lifted the box out and opened it. Inside, a brass instrument shone in front of her flashlight. It had a tube you could look into on top, with two brass legs front and back and a curved something like a ruler on the bottom. She looked at the inside cover of the box.

"Professional sextant, Boston, Mass.," she read. "Sextant, huh?" she said aloud. "I know what that is. That's the instrument sailors used to tell where they were at sea by comparing certain stars to the horizon. Captain Morgan would be proud of me," she added with a grin.

She put the sextant back in the box and set it aside. "What else do we have in here?" she asked aloud. Below the sextant, she found a stack of several small flags of different colors. *Wonder what these are for?* she thought.

At the very bottom of the trunk, she found something wrapped up in cloth. She pulled it out and discovered that it was heavy and cold. She carefully unwrapped it. The bundle became two. She set the small bundle down on the floor and unwrapped the other. What she discovered sent an electric jolt of fear into her.

It was a gun. Glowing in the light of the flashlight was a large, heavy revolver. *I wonder if this is the gun Captain Morgan used for any of the bad things he did.*

DeeDee didn't know if it was loaded. But she knew enough about guns that she should leave it alone. She carefully rewrapped it and set it aside. The smaller wrapped bundle turned out to be bullets for the gun. She rewrapped them quickly.

There was nothing else to be seen in the trunk. DeeDee carefully put everything back in the trunk the way it had been originally. She was just putting the clothes back in their place when she heard something scratching and crawling around behind her.

"Who's there!" she hissed, grabbing her flashlight and shining it toward the sound. At first she saw nothing, and she felt the hairs on the back of her neck stand up. Then she saw it.

A huge rat ran from one corner across the edge of the attic and disappeared into a hole.

Her heart raced in her chest for a minute, but then she realized that the rat was gone. "I hope it's gone for good," she said in a loud voice. Then she saw something gleaming in the corner.

Closing the lid of the trunk, DeeDee turned and walked toward the corner where she had seen the rat. Her heart started pounding again, but it didn't stop her from looking in the corner. Something was there, something shiny. And she had an idea what it might be.

DeeDee's hands were shaking when she reached the corner, but the wobbling light showed a big pile of shredded paper. "I was right," she said out loud. "It's a rat's nest. And it's a big one!" Bits of colored cloth, sticks, spoons, and buttons were piled in the center of the nest. And right in the middle of it was Jenny's watch.

"Well!" DeeDee said aloud, "that rat must have been the thief all along." She looked closer and found the missing key to the front door, still on its small chain, lying next to Jenny's watch.

Just as she reached for the key and the watch, she heard a squeaking noise behind her. Startled, she swung her flashlight toward the sound. The front of the flashlight crashed against the boards by her head and shattered.

DeeDee was suddenly surrounded by darkness.

CHAPTER

Meeting Henry

"It was a scary ride," Jenny called up the elevator shaft. "But I'm OK."

Just a few seconds after those words were spoken, the light shining down the elevator shaft disappeared, leaving Jenny alone in the dark. *I should have told DeeDee how scared I am*, Jenny thought as she shivered. *But that's silly*, she reminded herself. *What good would that do? She's all the way in the attic. She can't do anything to help me right now.*

What was it that DeeDee said at the end? she asked herself. *Jesus and His angels would watch over us. That's what she said.*

"I sure wish I had some sort of light," she said out loud. Her voice echoed in the darkness. But it reminded her of a verse in the Bible they had learned as a memory verse in the Shoebox. *God's Word, the Bible, is a lamp to my feet and a light to my path* .She talked out loud again. "If I found DeeDee's family Bible down here, I would have a light and a sword!"

She had to giggle a little at the idea of her swinging a Bible at a rat or using it to see in a corner. But she did feel better knowing that God's Word said that Jesus and His angels would be with her. "And the Bible really is like a light," she said out loud. "It can show you where to step to solve the problems in your life."

She took a deep breath then took a small step forward. She felt a cold solid wall in front of her. "It feels like cement," she decided. "It must be the basement wall. And if that's the basement wall, then all I have to do is follow it around the wall and eventually I will either find the steps out of here or the light switch," she said.

Jenny felt along the cold wall, both hands hugging the cold concrete. Her left shin bumped against what felt like it might be a step. She stepped up onto it. "It's solid, but it feels like it's covered with dirt or a lot of dust," she said out loud as she reached down to feel the surface with her hands. "It's not steps—it's a long sloping board like a ramp. And it's too steep to try to walk up. I wonder what that is."

As Jenny spoke, her feet slipped out from under her. She slid on her back down the ramp and fell into some more of the dirt or dust. It flew up into her face. She coughed a little and tried to wipe it away.

"*Ugh*. Gross," she said as she sat on the floor. Sitting there, she felt around her. There were boards on either side, as if she were sitting in a sandbox. Her hand touched a smooth rock surface and then another. Then she realized were she was.

"It's a coal bin," she said to herself. "The place where they stored the coal that was burned in the old coal furnace this house must have had." She felt the edge of the coal bin and climbed out. The next thing she felt was another knock on the shins. "Ow! I wish I would stop that."

But this time was different. She reached down and felt a flat board by her knees. A little higher, she felt another board and then another.

Her heart skipped a beat. *Are these the steps out?* she asked silently. After a moment, she stepped up onto the first board. With one arm in front of her face and the other one reaching for the next step, Jenny took a step forward and up, then another and another. Suddenly she felt something dragging against her face.

"*Ugh*, more cobwebs," she said, trying to brush them away. Suddenly, she froze. "Wait a minute. This isn't a cobweb—it's a string! And I can only think of one good reason for a string to be hanging from the ceiling down here." She tugged on the string then blinked.

Bright, beautiful light filled the basement. One single light bulb dangled from two wires on the ceiling. One bulb and the electricity that powered it changed Jenny's world. She felt like laughing and crying at the same time!

Jenny sat on the wooden steps and put her head in her hands. "Thank You, Jesus," she whispered.

One look at the door at the top of the steps and she knew that it was locked on the outside. *But that's OK*, she decided. *I'll be happy to wait for DeeDee, now that the light is on.*

Jenny sat waiting for a long time on those

steps and looked around her. The dumbwaiter lay in a broken heap across from her. Between it and her were the coal bin and the coal chute that she had stumbled over.

To her left, a workbench stood against the other wall. "Someone has been working there," Jenny decided. "And not long ago." Curls of new shaved wood were still on the floor around it. Some bright metal had been cut with tin snips, and an odd piece still lay on one corner. Something had been drawn on a piece of paper that lay to one side.

A huffing noise made Jenny look up. On the far end of the basement, Jenny saw a fire light behind a glass plate. *That must be the gas furnace*, Jenny thought. Behind it, she could see the old coal furnace it had replaced.

The basement was pretty big. But something about it was odd. It went back a long way on the right where the two furnaces stood. However, on the left, a wooden wall came down from the ceiling to the floor. She looked at that wall very carefully. Something was wrong with it, but she couldn't tell what it was. Finally, she had to get up and look more closely.

"That's it," she decided, as she bent down to

look near the floor. "The wall comes down nearly to the floor, but it's not attached there. It's like the wall is just a wooden curtain built to hide something."

Jenny looked around the basement again. "This wall is hiding one corner of the basement. Why would someone want to hide something down here?"

She looked at the wooden sheet that covered the end nearest her. Old nails held it in place. "I can do something to find out, if I can find a hammer—like the one right there on the workbench."

She grabbed the big claw hammer and worked the claw in under the edge of the sheet of wood. With a mighty tug, the board came loose. Jenny got her fingers under the edge of the board and pulled it the rest of the way free.

When she saw what was behind the wood, Jenny almost forgot to breathe. Then she grinned.

"Hello, Henry," she said.

CHAPTER 9

Rescue!

It's a funny thing about darkness, DeeDee thought. *When it's really dark, your eyes slowly get better and better at seeing with very little light. Right now, I am very glad that the moon is shining in through the attic window like a pale yellow flashlight beam.*

DeeDee stood still for a long time after she broke her flashlight. First, it was because she was too scared to move. The darkness made the little noises around her more frightening. Every creak, squeak, or scratch made her wonder what—or who—had made it.

After a few minutes, her heart stopped racing, and she was able to think more clearly. As her eyes adjusted to the darkness, she saw something that made her want to kick herself. In the very center of the room was a ladder. The ladder was folded up into three sections. She had missed it before. As DeeDee looked at it, she realized that the ladder was attached to a trap door. *All I have to do*, she decided, *is push the trap door down and the ladder will unfold.*

DeeDee was tired of the attic. "I need to rescue Jenny in the basement," she announced out loud. She walked over to the folded ladder and trap door and pushed down on it. Nothing happened. She looked at the trap door in the pale moonlight. *"Why won't it go down?"*

She couldn't see any reason why it wouldn't. "Maybe it just takes more weight to push it open." She thought out loud. She carefully stepped on the edge of the trap door. It still refused to move. She put both feet on it. Nothing. She hopped up and down. "Why won't this trap door open?"

She looked around the attic. If I could find something else to stack up here, that might make it heavy enough to push open. She snapped her fingers. "Captain Morgan's chest! If I drag it over here and set it on the trap door, maybe it will add enough weight to open the trap door."

She crept through the dark and grabbed the heavy chest by a leather strap that still hung from one side. She pulled. The chest moved a little toward her. She pulled again. It slid a little farther. She grabbed the leather handle with both hands and pulled. The strap came off in her hands and she fell backward.

"This trunk is not going to get the better of me," she said out loud. She stepped behind the chest and gave it a shove toward the trap door. "Captain Morgan was a tough person, and so am I. I am getting out of here."

Ten sweating minutes later, DeeDee lifted the edge of the chest onto the trap door. She gave it a push until the heavy trunk sat on top of the folded ladder. She paused.

"It's not opening," DeeDee muttered. "What is wrong with this door?"

Then DeeDee noticed the metal latch that held the trap door shut. "What's wrong with me?" she asked out loud. Then she reached down and slid the brass latch to one side.

Boom! The trap door swung down, the ladder

folded out, and Captain Morgan's trunk fell eight feet to the floor below. The noise was as loud as a thunderstorm.

"Yes!" DeeDee said. "I opened it!"

"What in the world is going on here?" a voice asked from the floor below her. DeeDee looked down to see her mother wrapped in her robe staring up at her.

Now that she wasn't scared anymore, Jenny was getting bored. *For all I know, DeeDee went back to bed, and everyone else is still asleep.* Then she heard a noise behind her. Keys jingled outside the double doors at the top of the stairs. Then one key was inserted into the padlock, and it clicked open. A blast of cold air came in as the double doors pulled back.

"DeeDee! Mrs. Adams! Am I glad to see you!" Jenny ran up the stairs toward her two rescuers.

"What happened to you!" Mrs. Adams said. "Just look at you. DeeDee! Is this some sort of joke or something?"

Jenny stopped where she was, halfway up the stairs. It hadn't occurred to her to think about how she looked. She looked at her hands and then at the rest of her body. Black. Everything on her was black. As she looked down at her feet, a fine shower of coal dust fell from her hair to the floor.

DeeDee started to laugh. "If I didn't know who you were . . . I wouldn't know who you were," she said.

Jenny laughed too. "Are you all right?" Mrs. Adams finally asked. She stepped down and pulled a tissue out of her robe pocket. She brushed Jenny's face with it. Jenny immediately realized that her face was covered with black coal dust.

"*Ugh*," she said as Mrs. Adams kept wiping her face. "Did you find anything up there?" she asked DeeDee.

DeeDee grinned in response, reached into her pocket, and pulled out something. She handed Jenny's new watch to her.

"Now I know why you don't like rats," DeeDee said.

Jenny's mouth fell open. "A rat had my watch?"

"It must have been a pack rat," Mrs. Adams said. "They collect things, especially shiny things."

"Could that rat have stolen the Family Treasure—the Bible, I mean?" DeeDee asked.

"No, the Bible would have been too heavy and too large," Mrs. Adams said. "It possibly could have taken a page or two at a time, or chewed it to pieces."

"We weren't away long enough for it to have chewed the Bible up, or stolen it a page at a time," DeeDee said.

"I think I know where the Bible is," Jenny said. "But first, I want to introduce you two to someone." She took the tissue and wiped her hands with it as she walked down the stairs. DeeDee and Mrs. Adams followed her across the concrete floor to the corner where the boards had been torn away.

"DeeDee, Mrs. Adams, meet Henry." Jenny held the boards back so DeeDee and her mom could see the black antique car that stood behind the board curtain.

"It's a Model T Ford," Mrs. Adams said in surprise. "Girls, this was one of the first automobiles made in this country." She looked back at the old car. "This thing is ancient." Mrs. Adams looked at Jenny. "But how did you know this car was called Henry?"

Jenny pointed to dust that had collected on the hood of the car. The word *Henry* had been traced in the dust by someone's finger.

"I think someone—probably Grandma—wrote his name on him a long time ago," DeeDee said.

"So this is Henry," Mrs. Adams said.

"I wish we could talk to Grandma about him," DeeDee said.

"Well, why don't you?" Mrs. Adams said.

"What?" DeeDee and Jenny asked. "Is she all right?"

"She's feeling fine, and she's awake upstairs," Mrs. Adams said. "She's asked to talk to you."

Grandma's Story

"Come here, children," Grandma Adams said, reaching out from her bed.

DeeDee and Jenny approached Grandma Adams slowly; DeeDee's hair was full of cobwebs, and Jenny was black from head to foot from coal dust.

"Have you been having fun exploring this old house?" Grandma asked. She chuckled and brushed the cobwebs from DeeDee's hair.

DeeDee grinned and nodded. "This house doesn't give up its secrets easily, but we learned a thing or two about it."

"Such as?" Grandma raised one eyebrow.

"We found your diary," Jenny said. "I hope you don't mind us looking at it."

"Diary?" Grandma said. "I don't remember having a—ahh yes." She smiled slowly, remembering. "That was a really long time ago."

"We were trying to find out the truth about Captain Morgan," DeeDee said.

"And did you?" Grandma asked.

DeeDee told Grandma about finding the hidden passageway and following it to Captain Morgan's room.

"And we found your initials and those of others in the passageway," Jenny said.

"Those other initials were there a long time before you were born," said Grandma. "The man who owned the boardinghouse before my Daddy—Hansen, I think his name was—used it to hide runaway slaves before the war between the states. That's the Civil War, I think you call it."

DeeDee nudged Jenny. "I told you."

"Is that how your daddy snuck Captain Morgan in and out of the boardinghouse?" Jenny asked.

Grandma nodded. "I would use that passageway to visit him every night. That is, until he left us that night in August."

"Oh, you mean the night he was killed," DeeDee said.

"Killed? Goodness, no," Grandma laughed. "My daddy would come in and read to him from the Bible every night. And every night after Daddy left, Captain Morgan would ask me about what Daddy had read.

"One night we were talking about John, chapter 3, where Jesus told Nicodemus that he must be born again. I was explaining it to Captain Morgan, when he up and let out a wail. I thought he hurt himself, but then he started crying. I asked him what was the matter.

" 'Abigail,' he said to me. 'I am not the man I need to be. Those words cut through me like a sword.' "

DeeDee looked at Jenny. "The sword of the Spirit!" DeeDee said. "Now I know what Mrs. Shue meant. That's how the Bible is like a sword!"

"Captain Morgan decided right then and there to give himself over entirely to Jesus," Grandma continued. "We went downstairs and woke Daddy up. Daddy and two of his deacons took Captain Morgan down to the river."

"And drowned him?" Jenny asked weakly.

"No! Baptized him, child. They put that mean old man under the water, and his meanness just washed on down to the ocean. The man who came up out of the water belonged to Jesus!"

"That's what you meant when you said that he was with Jesus," DeeDee said. "But what happened to him after that? I found his trunk up in the attic."

"And I found Henry down in the base, uh, cellar," Jenny said.

Grandma laughed. "Oh, Henry! How I loved that car! Captain Morgan left that night and headed back to Mississippi to do what he could for that family he had hurt so badly years before. He said he was a new man, and he didn't want anything to do with the things that belonged to the old man, the mean old man that was washed down the river."

"So, in a sense, the old Captain Morgan was washed away down the river," DeeDee said.

Grandma nodded. "Captain Morgan didn't have any money to pay Daddy for putting him up and taking care of him for so long. So when he left, he gave Daddy his brand new Model T

Ford. In those days, if a Black man was seen with something as nice as a new car, he would be beaten, or worse. Daddy and his deacons moved the car into the cellar to protect it and to hide it. He never got around to taking it out."

Grandma leaned back in her bed and sighed. "I really loved that car."

DeeDee looked at her grandmother then at Jenny. "There's one more mystery that hasn't been solved. What happened to the family Bible?"

Jenny winked. "Ask your brother."

Everyone turned and looked at Marcus, who stood in the doorway. Marcus got red and shook his head.

"Why is everyone looking at me?" he asked.

Jenny grinned. "You left for your errand, then came back and took the Bible when DeeDee and I walked out to the car."

"What are you talking about?" Marcus answered, trying to look innocent.

"Then you took it down to the cellar—I mean basement," Jenny said.

"I what?"

"And you did something to it down there." Jenny said.

Marcus looked at Jenny, then DeeDee, then

his mother and grandmother.

"Tell the truth, Marcus," Mrs. Adams said.

Marcus paused then exhaled loudly. "All right, you caught me. DeeDee, Jenny, you two detectives are too smart for your own good."

He stepped out of the room into the hallway. After a minute, he came back with something in his hands. It was a wooden box that had been trimmed in copper foil. Marcus carried it over to Grandma and held it as if it were a treasure. As Grandma looked at it, sure enough, on the cover it said "Family Treasure" in copper.

Grandma took the box from Marcus and held it in her lap. She opened it carefully. Inside was the Family Bible.

"Everyone was so worried about it getting damaged," Marcus said quietly. "I wanted to do something to protect it. I wanted it to be a surprise."

Grandma Adams looked down at the Bible then up at Marcus. "You're a jewel, Marcus," she said, cupping her hands around his face and kissing him.

"Imagine that," Jenny said to DeeDee.

"What?" DeeDee asked.

"Swords are used to protect people," she said.

"Marcus found a way to protect this Sword."

"After all the Bible has done for my family, don't you think it deserves a little protection?" DeeDee answered.

Jenny smiled. "You're right. I'm so glad you invited me to stay here with you, DeeDee. This has been about the most interesting weekend of my life. You don't think there are any more mysteries in this house, do you?"

DeeDee didn't answer. She turned and looked at her grandmother.

Grandma Adams just smiled. "I don't suppose you two have learned everything about this house yet."

Now DeeDee smiled as she turned to Jenny. "Here we go again."